Robert Francis Harper, Leroy Waterman

Assyrian and Babylonian letters belonging to the Kouyunjik

collections of the British museum

Robert Francis Harper, Leroy Waterman

Assyrian and Babylonian letters belonging to the Kouyunjik collections of the British museum

ISBN/EAN: 9783337283742

Printed in Europe, USA, Canada, Australia, Japan

Cover: Foto ©Andreas Hilbeck / pixelio.de

More available books at **www.hansebooks.com**

ASSYRIAN

AND

BABYLONIAN LETTERS

BELONGING TO

THE KOUYUNJIK COLLECTIONS OF THE BRITISH MUSEUM

BY

ROBERT FRANCIS HARPER, Ph.D

PROFESSOR OF THE SEMITIC LANGUAGES AND LITERATURES
IN THE UNIVERSITY OF CHICAGO

PART IX

THE UNIVERSITY OF CHICAGO PRESS

LUZAC AND CO., LONDON

1909

TO

MY FORMER TEACHER

FRIEDRICH DELITZSCH

PREFACE

In Part VIII, it was announced that Part IX would be an Index Volume, giving Lists of all the Proper Names, Officials, Divinities, Countries, Peoples, Cities, etc., found in Parts I–VIII, with references to their British Museum registration numbers and to the numbers which they bear in this Series. This Index Volume will appear as a later Part in the Series.

The present Part contains the texts of ninety-eight tablets. On seventy-four of these the name of the scribe is to be found; on twenty-four the name has been broken away. The headline is the reading of the name of the scribe found in the Letter over which it stands. The name of the person addressed is placed in the headline over two or three Letters in which the name of the scribe is broken away. No attempt has been made to classify Letters on which the names of the scribes are broken away, as this more naturally falls within the province of the commentary.

Index I is a Table of Contents. Index II is a list of the tablets arranged according to their numbers in the Kouyunjik Collections. Index III is a list of tablets published in Parts I–IX, the superior numeral indicating the number of the Part. Compare Part VIII for Index IV, which gives a list of the tablets published in Parts I–VIII arranged according to the names of the Scribes, with references to their British Museum registration numbers, and to the numbers which they bear in this Edition.

Twenty-seven or twenty-eight of the Letters contained in this Part have been published by previous editors, and I am much indebted to them for their copies. To WINCKLER, a fellow student under SCHRADER, I am especially indebted for his carefully prepared copies of twenty-three Letters, namely, KK. Nos. 233, 844, 894, 1146, 1238, 1245 (to which, since his publication, 83-1-18, 107 has been joined), 1269, 1287, 1355, 1459, 1542, 1580, 1610, 1621*b*, 1881, 1895, 2645, 2701*a*, 2889, 4287, 4447, 4724 and 4776. I have not been able, however, to accept all his readings, and I may also say that I do not expect scholars to accept all mine. Many of the tablets are broken and difficult to read, and in such it is often impossible to form a connected text. Again, in the Letters there are as many different handwritings as there were scribes. Hence, there will be many places where scholars may differ from my readings. In the final collation of all the Letter texts, I myself hope to be able to decide the readings of many passages, about which there is, to my mind, still some uncertainty.

I am much honoured by the attention shown to this class of literature, and I wish to state here that as soon as the texts are published they become public property, and anyone may use them for any purpose he may wish. This work by my fellow students will in no way interfere with my original plan as described in Part I and again in Part IV, and I see no reason to depart from this plan as outlined seventeen years ago. Hence, I shall continue to publish the texts until the *Corpus Epistolarum* is completed, and again I express the hope that the Parts will appear more frequently in the future than in the past.

Part X is in preparation.

I wish especially to acknowledge my obligations to DR. E. WALLIS BUDGE, the Keeper of the Department of Egyptian and Assyrian Antiquities, British Museum, for

his courtesy and for the great assistance which he has
afforded me in the preparation of these Parts. It was at
his suggestion that the work was originally undertaken, and
without his sympathy and assistance it would not have been
possible to carry it out. I am indebted also to the other
members of the Department, MESSRS. KING, HALL, SCOTT-
MONCRIEFF and HANDCOCK for their unfailing courtesy. To
MR. KING I am also grateful for suggestions as to the
reading of several signs.

To my former teacher, PROFESSOR FRIEDRICH DELITZSCH,
of the University of Berlin, I have the honour to dedicate
this Volume.

ROBERT FRANCIS HARPER

THE STUDENTS' ROOM,
THE DEPARTMENT OF EGYPTIAN AND
ASSYRIAN ANTIQUITIES, THE BRITISH MUSEUM,
November the fifth, 1909.

[877.] K. 6.

OBVERSE.

3.

6.

9.

12.

15.

EDGE.

REVERSE.

3.

6.

9.

12.

15.

OBVERSE.

3.

6.

9.

12.

15.

18.

21.

REVERSE.

[879.] K. 359.

OBV. (cuneiform text lines 1-24)

1. 𒀭𒁉 𒀸𒌐𒌋𒌋 𒅖𒂟𒌅 𒂖𒐊 𒀜𒈾 𒋼𒌋𒐊

2. 𒐊 𒀭𒐊𒌋 𒀭𒊏𒐊𒀜 𒈾 𒋼𒌋 𒀭 𒋝𒈬𒐊 𒌋𒀸𒐊

3. 𒐊 𒀭𒐊 𒅖𒐊 𒂟𒈪 𒌋𒅖 𒂖𒐊 𒂖𒐊 𒅖𒐊 𒀜 𒐊 𒐊 𒐊𒐊

4. 𒀭𒅂 𒌋𒐊 𒂖𒐊 𒀊𒐊𒐊 𒅖𒂟 𒂖𒐊 𒐊𒐊 𒀸𒐊 𒀜 𒈨 𒀜𒐊 𒐊 𒌋𒌋

5. 𒐊 𒌋𒐊 𒐊 𒌋𒌋 𒂖 𒌋𒐊 𒅖𒀭 𒂖𒌋 𒋝 𒅖𒀜 𒀊𒂟 ▓▓▓

6. 𒀭𒀜𒐊 𒌋𒐊𒀜 𒀜𒈾 𒋼𒌋 𒂖𒐊 𒂖𒐊 𒀊𒐊𒐊 𒂟 𒌋 𒀭 𒂖𒐊▓

7. 𒅖𒐊𒐊 𒅖𒂟𒐊 𒐊 𒀜𒅖 𒂖 𒅖𒐊𒌋 𒂖𒌋 𒂖𒐊𒐊𒐊 𒌋𒀜 𒀊 𒀜𒌋 𒐊 𒌋𒌋

8. 𒀜 𒐊𒐊 𒂖𒐊 𒌅𒌋 𒐊 𒌋𒐊 𒌋 𒂖𒌋 𒀜 𒀜𒐊𒌋 𒅖𒐊 𒐊𒀜 𒐊 𒌋𒌋

9. 𒂖𒐊 𒂖𒐊 𒀜𒐊 𒌋𒐊 𒐊 𒐊 𒐊 𒅖𒐊 𒅖𒂟𒐊 𒅖𒐊𒌋 𒐊 𒌋𒀜 𒀊 𒀜𒌋 𒀜 𒌋𒌋

10. 𒐊 𒌋𒐊𒀜 𒀊𒐊𒐊 𒅖𒐊 𒂖𒀜 𒂟𒐊 𒂖𒌋𒌋 𒂖𒐊 𒂟𒈨

11. 𒂖𒐊𒐊 𒐊𒌋 𒂖𒐊 𒂖𒐊 𒀜 𒀊𒌋 𒀊𒐊 𒋼 𒌋 𒀜𒅖𒐊 𒐊 𒐊𒌋 𒐊𒐊▓

12. 𒌋 𒀭𒐊𒐊 𒐊𒂖 𒐊𒌋 𒀜 𒌋 𒅖𒐊𒐊 𒈨 𒀜 𒌋 ▓▓ 𒂖𒀜 𒅖𒐊𒐊

13. 𒌋 𒐊𒐊 𒂖𒐊 𒀭 𒅖𒐊𒐊 𒂖𒀜 𒐊𒐊𒐊 𒂟𒈨 𒂖𒐊𒐊 𒅖𒐊 𒐊𒐊

14. 𒂖𒐊𒐊 𒐊𒌋 𒂖 𒂖𒐊 𒂟 𒀜 𒀊𒐊 𒅖𒐊𒐊 𒀜𒌋 𒐊 𒀜 𒐊𒌋

15. 𒐊 𒀜𒂖𒌋 𒐊𒐊 𒀜 𒅖𒐊𒌋 𒀭 𒐊 𒌋 𒅖𒐊𒐊 𒐊𒐊 𒂟𒐊

16. 𒀭 𒀭𒐊𒐊𒐊 𒅖𒂟𒐊 𒂖𒐊 𒂟𒈨 𒀜 𒂖𒐊𒐊 𒐊𒌋 𒂖𒐊 𒂖𒐊 𒀭𒌋𒐊

17. 𒂖𒐊 𒂖𒐊 𒀜 𒀜 𒅖𒐊 𒂖𒐊 𒐊𒌋 𒐊 𒀊 𒂖𒐊 𒀜𒅖𒐊𒐊▓

18. 𒀜𒐊𒀊 𒐊𒂟 𒂖𒐊 𒐊 𒀊 𒀜 𒂖 𒀜𒀜 𒂖𒐊 𒂖𒐊𒐊 𒂖𒐊𒐊

19. 𒀜 𒀭𒐊𒐊 𒐊𒐊 𒐊𒌋 𒅖𒐊𒌋 𒂖𒐊 𒀜𒅖 𒀜𒐊𒀊 𒀊𒐊𒐊 𒂖𒐊 𒀜𒐊 𒐊𒈨 𒐊

20. 𒂖𒐊 𒀜 𒅖𒐊 𒐊𒌋 𒐊𒐊 𒀜 𒅖𒐊𒌋 𒂖𒐊𒐊 𒐊𒌋 𒐊

21. ▓▓▓ 𒌋𒌋 𒂖𒐊𒐊 𒀭 𒀜𒌋 𒐊𒌋 𒂟𒈨

22. 𒀜𒂖𒀜 𒂖𒈨 𒂖𒌋𒐊 𒐊𒌋 𒐊 𒐊𒈨 𒂖𒈨

23. 𒐊 𒐊𒐊 𒐊𒌋 𒌋 𒂖𒈨

24. 𒂖𒈨 𒐊 𒌋𒀜 𒐊𒌋 𒀭 𒌋𒐊 𒐊

25. 𒀭𒐊𒐊 𒂖 𒅖𒐊𒐊 𒂖𒐊 𒂖𒐊 ▓▓

REV.

1. ▓▓▓ 𒐊𒐊

2. 𒐊𒐊 𒐊𒌋𒀜 𒌋𒀜 𒐊𒌋(?)

3. 𒅖𒐊𒐊 𒐊𒌋 𒂖𒐊 𒐊𒐊 𒀜𒈨(?)

4. 𒐊 𒂖𒐊 𒂖𒐊𒐊 𒂖𒐊(?) 𒌋 𒂟

5. 𒌋𒀜 𒂖𒐊𒐊 𒂖𒐊(?)

6. 𒂖𒐊 𒂖𒐊 𒌋 𒂖𒐊 𒂖𒐊(?) 𒂖𒐊𒐊(?) 𒀜𒈨(?)

7. 𒐊𒀊 𒐊𒌋 𒌋 𒂖𒐊

8. 𒐊 𒐊 𒌋

9. 𒂖𒐊 𒂖𒐊 𒀜𒌋𒌋 𒅖𒐊 𒂖𒈨 𒀜𒐊𒌋 𒐊 𒌋 𒀜𒈨 𒌋𒌋 𒌋 𒐊𒌋 𒐊

OBVERSE.

[880.] **K. 473** (*continued*).

REVERSE.

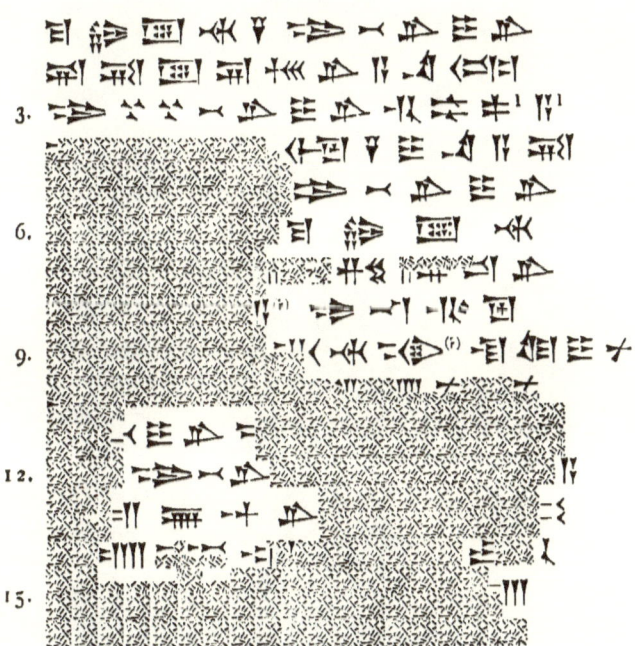

³·

⁶·

⁹·

¹²·

¹⁵·

LEFT-HAND EDGE.

---

[1] Written over an erasure.

[881.] K. 489.[1]

OBVERSE.

3.

6.

9.

12.

REVERSE.

3.

---

[1] This tablet is disintegrating.

[882.] 82-5-22, 102.

OBVERSE.

3.

6.

9.

12.

REVERSE.

[883.] K. 500.

OBVERSE.

3.

6.

9.

12.

15.

18.

21.

EDGE. 24.

¹ Defaced, and hence very doubtful.
² Written over an erasure.

6 G

REVERSE.

［cuneiform text］

3. ［cuneiform text］

6. ［cuneiform text］
(erasure) ［cuneiform text］

9. ［cuneiform text］

12. ［cuneiform text］

15. ［cuneiform text］

---

[1] Defaced, and hence very doubtful.
[2] Partly erased, and hence doubtful.

[884.] K. 510.

Obverse.

3.

6.

9.

12.

15.

EDGE. 18.

---

[1] Written over an erasure.

[884.] **K. 510** (*continued*).

Reverse.

3.

6.

9.

12.

15.

18.

Edge.

21.

[885.] K. 521.[1]

Obverse.

⟨cuneiform⟩
⟨cuneiform⟩
3. ⟨cuneiform⟩
⟨cuneiform⟩
⟨cuneiform⟩
6. ⟨cuneiform⟩
⟨cuneiform⟩
⟨cuneiform⟩
9. ⟨cuneiform⟩
⟨cuneiform⟩
⟨cuneiform⟩
12. ⟨cuneiform⟩
⟨cuneiform⟩
⟨cuneiform⟩
15. ⟨cuneiform⟩
⟨cuneiform⟩
⟨cuneiform⟩
18. ⟨cuneiform⟩
⟨cuneiform⟩
⟨cuneiform⟩
21. ⟨cuneiform⟩
⟨cuneiform⟩
⟨cuneiform⟩
24. ⟨cuneiform⟩

Edge. ⟨cuneiform⟩
⟨cuneiform⟩
27. ⟨cuneiform⟩

[1] This tablet is disintegrating.

[885.] **K. 521** (*continued*).

REVERSE.

3.

6.

9.

12.

15.

18.

21.

24.

EDGE.

LEFT-HAND EDGE.

27.

---

[1] Defaced, and hence doubtful.

[886.] K. 605.

OBVERSE.

3.

6.

9.

12.

15.

EDGE.

18.

REVERSE.

3.

[887.] K. 648.

OBVERSE.

3.

6.

9.

12.

15.

18.

REVERSE.

3.

6.

[888.] K. 658.

OBVERSE.

3.

6. (erasure.)

9.

12.

15.

REVERSE.

3.

[889.] K. 675.

OBVERSE.

3.

6.

9.

12.

REVERSE.

3.

6.

9.

6 H 2

[890.]   K. 676.

OBVERSE.

    𒌋 ...

3. ...

6. ...

9. ...

12. ...

[890.]   **K. 676** (*continued*).

REVERSE.

3.

6.

9.

12.

15.

EDGE.

18.

LEFT-HAND EDGE.

[891.] K. 1079.

OBVERSE.

```
       𒁹𒁹 𒌷𒁹 𒉌𒈨𒌍 𒄿𒅆 𒉌𒈨𒌍
       𒄿𒁹 𒄿𒁹 𒁹 𒀸𒈦𒊩 𒄿𒅆
3.  𒁹𒁹 𒌗 𒀸𒈦𒊩 𒁹𒁹𒁹 𒉌𒈨𒌍 𒄿𒅆 𒉌𒈨𒌍
 .  𒁹 𒁹𒁹(?) 𒁹𒁹 𒁹𒁹𒁹 𒀼𒁹 𒌗 𒉌
    𒄿 𒄿𒁹𒁹 𒁹𒁹 𒄿𒈨𒁹(?) 𒊩 𒁹𒁹 𒁹𒁹 𒉌𒈨𒌍(?)
6.  [          ] 𒄿 𒄿𒈨𒁹 𒀹 𒁹𒁹𒁹 𒌗 𒀼
    [          ]    𒄿 𒄿𒈨𒁹 𒊩 𒌷𒄿
    [          ]        𒄿𒈨𒁹 𒁹 𒐊𒁹
9.  [                              ] 𒐊𒁹
```

REVERSE.

```
    [                                  ]
    [      ] 𒐈 𒀼 𒁹𒉌      𒌍
3.  𒁹𒁹 𒌷𒁹𒁹𒁹
    𒄴 𒉌𒈨𒌍
    𒁹 𒁹𒄿 𒄿𒁹
6.  𒁍𒁹 𒀹𒁹𒁹
    𒌷𒈨𒌍 𒌦
    𒉌𒈨𒌍𒈨𒌍
9.  𒌦𒁹  𒁹
```

𒁹 𒂖 𒀪 𒐊

[892.] K. 684.

OBVERSE.

3.

6.

9.

12.

15.

EDGE.

[892.] **K. 684** (*continued*).

REVERSE.

3.

6.

9.

12.

15.

EDGE. 18.

21.

LEFT-HAND EDGE.

(erasure)

24.

[893.] K. 8409.

OBVERSE.

3.

6.

9.

REVERSE.

3.

6.

9.

12.

15.

EDGE.

18.

LEFT-HAND EDGE.

[894.] K. 685.

Obverse.

    [cuneiform]

    [cuneiform]

3. [cuneiform]

    [cuneiform]

    [cuneiform]

6. [cuneiform]

    [cuneiform]

    [cuneiform]

9. [cuneiform]

    [cuneiform]

    [cuneiform]

12. [cuneiform]

    [cuneiform]

Edge. [cuneiform]

15. [cuneiform]

Reverse.

    [cuneiform]

    [cuneiform]

3. [cuneiform]

    [cuneiform]

    [cuneiform]

6. [cuneiform]

    [cuneiform]

    [cuneiform]

9. [cuneiform]

    [cuneiform]

    [cuneiform]

12. [cuneiform]

    [cuneiform]

    [cuneiform]

Edge. 15. [cuneiform]

[895.] K. 772.

OBVERSE.

3.

6.

9.

EDGE.

REVERSE.

3.

6.

9.

EDGE.

[896.] K. 832ᵇ.

Obverse.

3.

6.

9.

12.

15.

18.

21.

Edge.

24.

¹ Written over an erasure.

[896.] **K. 832ᵇ** (*continued*).

REVERSE.

3. (era|sure)

6.

9.

12.

15.

18.

LEFT-HAND EDGE.

¹ Written over an erasure.

[897.] K. 835.

Obverse.

3.

6.

9.

12.

Edge. 15.

Reverse.

3.

6.

9.

12.

15.

[898.]   K. 8301.

OBVERSE.

3.

6.

REVERSE.

3.

6.

EDGE.

9.

LEFT-HAND EDGE.

[899.] K. 844.

OBVERSE.

3.

6.

9.

12.

REVERSE.

3.

6.

9.

12.

EDGE.

15.

[900.] K. 894.

Obverse.

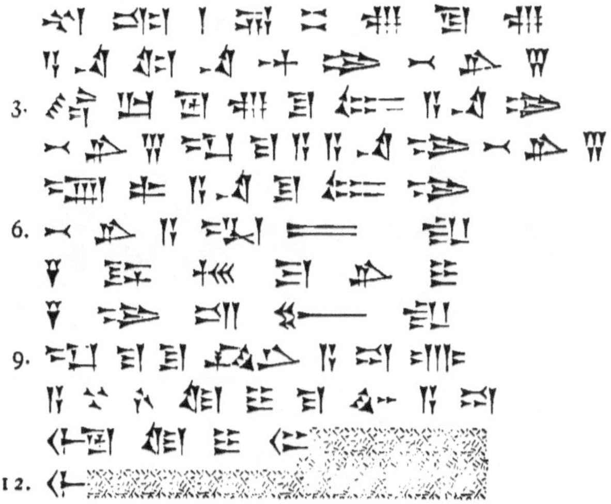

Edge.

Reverse completely broken away.

[901.] K. 926.

OBVERSE.

3.

6.

9.

EDGE.

REVERSE.

3.

6.

9.

EDGE.

12.

6 K

[902.] **K. 1046.**

OBVERSE.

〖cuneiform text — line 1〗
〖cuneiform text — line 2〗
3. 〖cuneiform text — line 3〗
〖cuneiform text — line 4〗
〖cuneiform text — line 5〗
6. 〖cuneiform text — line 6〗
〖cuneiform text — line 7〗
〖cuneiform text — line 8〗

REVERSE not inscribed.

[903.]   K. 1071.

OBVERSE.

3.

6.

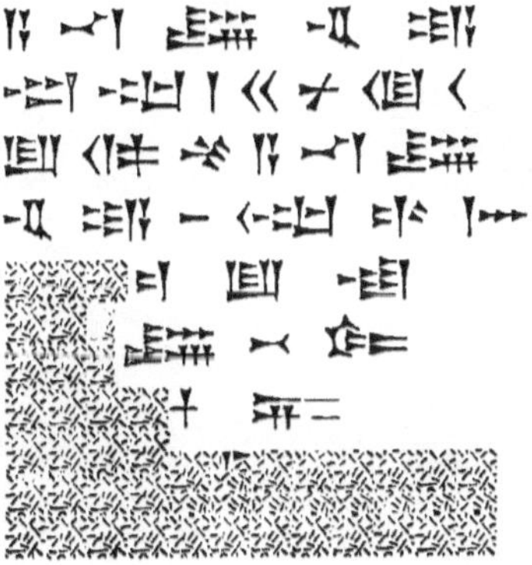

REVERSE.

3.

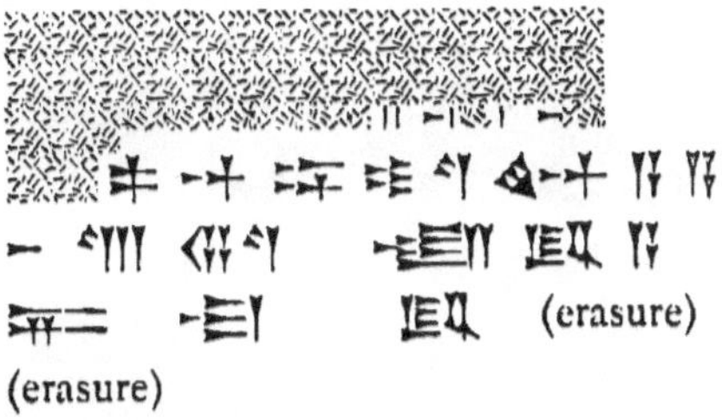

(erasure)

(erasure)

[904.] K. 13027.

OBVERSE.

3. 〔cuneiform〕

REVERSE broken away.

[905.] K. 13120.

OBVERSE.

3. 〔cuneiform〕

REVERSE broken away.

[906.] K. 1146.

OBVERSE.

3.

6.

9.

12.

REVERSE.

3.

6.

EDGE. 9.

LEFT-HAND EDGE.

12.

[907.] K. 1177.

OBVERSE.

𒊬𒄠 𒄷 𒁹 𒌋𒄠 𒋫𒁲𒊭 𒁲 𒈫

𒌋𒄠 𒁁 𒆠𒈠 𒄷 𒋫𒁲

3. 𒂍 𒅖 𒁹 𒌋𒄠 𒋫 𒁁 𒌋𒌋𒌋

𒌋𒂍 𒅖 𒁹 𒋫𒁲𒊭 𒄩𒁲 𒅆 𒈨 𒅖 𒌋𒌋

𒀀𒂍 𒁹 𒄷𒊬𒄠 𒀭 𒅖 𒌋𒌋

6. 𒌋𒄠 𒁕 𒋫 𒁲 𒁁 𒌋𒌋𒌋

𒅗𒈨 𒁷 𒇻

𒇻𒄭 𒊬𒁕 𒁷 𒁹

9. 𒄑 𒁲 𒅖𒅖 𒇻

𒌋𒄠 𒁲 𒁁 𒅖𒅖

𒀀𒂍 𒌋𒅆 𒈫 𒂍

12. ░░░𒁹 𒀉 𒄊░░░

EDGE.

𒇻 𒁁 𒄊░░░

REVERSE.

░░░𒋫░░░𒋽 𒁕 𒌋░░░

𒄷 𒁁 𒀭𒀯 𒅆───── 𒂍

[908.] K. 1188.

OBVERSE.

𒇽 ⤚𒁹 𒂄𒇻 ⤚𒈜 𒂍𒇻

⤚𒁹 ⤚𒂠 𒀭 ⤚𒐏 ⟨𒈨𒌋 ⊱ —

3. 𒉽 ⟨ ⟨𒉺𒉿 ⊱ 𒇽 ⤚𒁹 ⟪ ⤚𒐏 𒂍𒇻

𒇽 𒂍𒌋 ⟪ 𒇽 𒂍𒌋 ⟪

6. 𒐋

REVERSE completely broken away.

[909.] Bu. 91 5-9, 49.

OBVERSE.

𒇽 ⤚𒁹 𒂄𒇻   ⤚𒈜 𒂍𒇻

⤚𒁹 ⤚𒂠 𒀭 ⤚𒐏 ⟨𒈨𒌋 ⊱ —

3. 𒉽 ⟨𒉺𒉿 ⊱ 𒇽 ⤚𒁹 𒂄𒇻 ⤚𒈜 𒂍𒇻

⤚𒐏 ⤚𒁾 ⤚𒐏 ⟨𒊹𒁹 𒇽 ⤚𒁹 𒂄𒇻

⤚𒈜 𒂍𒇻   𒉽 𒐊 ⊱

6. ⤚𒐏 ⟪⟪ ⤚𒐏

9.

REVERSE.

[910.] K. 1194.

OBVERSE.

3.

6.

9.

12.

REVERSE.

3.

6.

9.

¹ Filled with silica, and hence doubtful.

[911.] K. 1215.

Obverse.

3.

6.

9.

Reverse completely broken away.

[912.] K. 1237.

Obverse.

3.

6.

9.

Edge. 12.

Rev.

3.

6.

9.

12.

Edge.

Left-hand Edge.

15.

---

[1] Written over an erasure.

[2] Written over an erasure; perhaps = 𒁹 𒅆𒌋 (erasure) 𒌋𒌋.

6 L 2

[913.] K. 1238.

OBVERSE.

REVERSE.

EDGE.

[914.] K. 1245 + 83–1–18, 107.

OBVERSE.

3.

6.

9.

12.

15.

18.

EDGE.

[914.] K. 1245 + 83-1-18, 107 (*continued*).

REVERSE.

[915.] K. 1269.

OBVERSE.

3.

6.

9.

12.

REVERSE.

3.

6.

9.

12.

[916.] **K. 1287.**

OBVERSE.

3.

6.

9.

12.

15.

EDGE.

¹ These signs have been badly defaced.

REVERSE.

3.

6.

9.

12.

15.

[1] This sign has been badly defaced.

[917.] K. 1355.

Obverse.

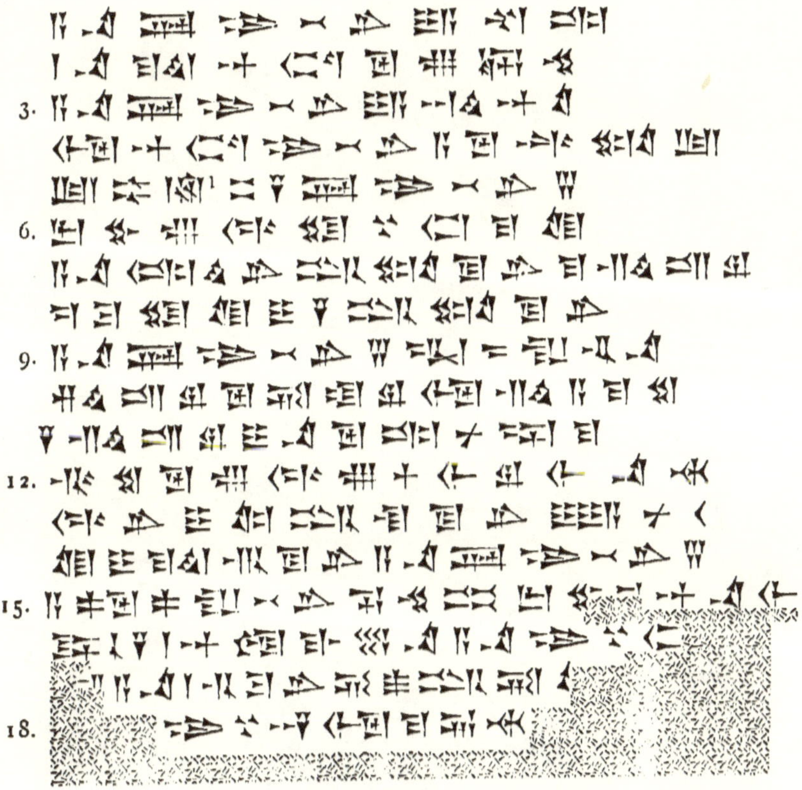

[1] So written.

[917.] **K. 1355** (*continued*).

REVERSE.

3.

6.

9.

12.

15.

[1] So written.

[918.] K. 1542.

Obverse.

3.

6.

9.

12.

15.

Reverse.

3.

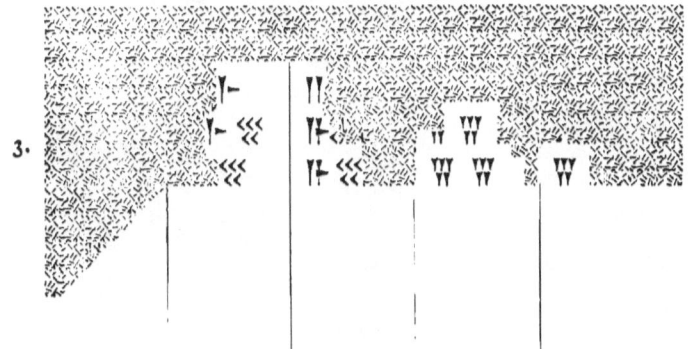

[919.] K. 1555.

OBVERSE.

3.

6.

REVERSE.

[920.] K. 1621ᵇ.

OBVERSE.

3.

6.

9.

12.

15.

18.

[920.] **K. 1621ᵇ** (*continued*).

REVERSE.

3.

6.

9.

12.

LEFT-HAND EDGE.

15.

[921.] K. 1889.

OBVERSE.

(cuneiform signs)

3. (cuneiform signs)

REVERSE.

Portions of five lines so effaced as
to be illegible

[1] Bezold restores ►⟨🖙, which is quite possible.

[922.] 82–5–22, 140.

OBVERSE.

(cuneiform signs)

3. (cuneiform signs)

6. (cuneiform signs)

NO REVERSE.

[923.] K. 2701a.

Obverse.

3.

6.

9.

12.

15.

18.

¹ Written [cuneiform].

[923.] K. 2701a. *(continued).*

REVERSE.

a unteralp

ˆ OBVERSE.

REVERSE completely broken away.

[925.]　K. 4287.

Obverse.

　　　　（cuneiform）

3.　　（cuneiform）

6.　　（cuneiform）

9.　　（cuneiform）

12.　　（cuneiform）

15.　　（cuneiform）

18.　　（cuneiform）

21.　　（cuneiform）

24.　　（cuneiform）

Edge.　　（cuneiform）

27.　　（cuneiform）

[925.] K. 4287 (*continued*).

REVERSE.

3.

6.

9.

12.

15.

OBVERSE.

3.

6.

9.

12.

15.

18.

REVERSE completely broken away.

[927.] K. 4522.

[928.] K. 5463.

Obverse.

3.

6.

9.

12.

15.

Reverse.

3.

6.

9.

(erasure)

12.

[929.] K. 5496.

Obverse.

Reverse.

Edge.

3.

6.

[930.] K. 5607.

OBVERSE.

〔cuneiform text〕

3. 〔cuneiform text〕

〔cuneiform text〕

〔cuneiform text〕

6. 〔cuneiform text〕

〔cuneiform text〕

〔cuneiform text〕

9. 〔cuneiform text〕

〔cuneiform text〕

〔cuneiform text〕

12. 〔cuneiform text〕

REVERSE.

〔cuneiform text〕

〔cuneiform text〕

3. 〔cuneiform text〕

〔cuneiform text〕

〔cuneiform text〕

6. 〔cuneiform text〕

〔cuneiform text〕

〔cuneiform text〕

9. 〔cuneiform text〕

〔cuneiform text〕

〔cuneiform text〕

EDGE. 12. 〔cuneiform text〕

〔cuneiform text〕

[931.] K. 7370.

OBVERSE.

REVERSE completely broken away.

[932.] K. 7487.

OBVERSE.

⟨cuneiform text⟩

3. ⟨cuneiform text⟩

6. ⟨cuneiform text⟩

REVERSE.

3. ⟨cuneiform text⟩

6. ⟨cuneiform text⟩

9. ⟨cuneiform text⟩

EDGE.

LEFT-HAND EDGE.

⟨cuneiform text⟩

[933.] K. 8855.

OBVERSE.

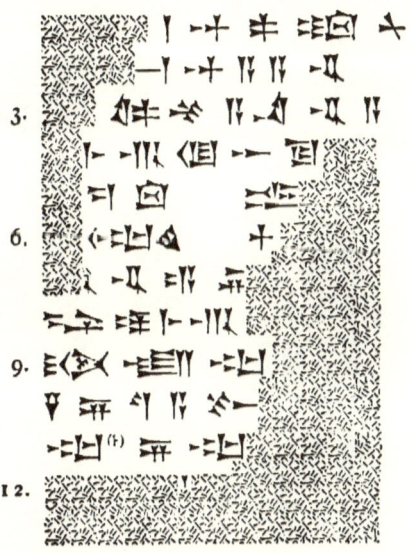

3.

6.

9.

12.

REVERSE.

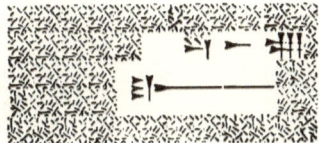

[934.] K. 12953.

OBVERSE.

REVERSE completely broken away.

[935.] K. 12969.

Obverse.

```
1. 𒌋 𒀭 𒈹 𒀭 𒌋𒌋 𒌋𒌋
2. 𒌈 𒈠 𒁴 𒁹
3. 𒀭𒁇𒌑𒍑 𒁹
   𒍑 𒁇 𒍑 𒌋 𒈹 𒀭 𒌋𒌋
   𒀀 𒌍 𒀜 𒁴𒀀
6. 𒌋 𒀭 𒈹 𒀭 𒌋𒌋 𒌋𒌋
   𒁴 𒈹 𒌋 𒁹
   𒀜 𒀜𒁴
9. 𒀭𒁹 𒈹
   𒀜
   𒁹
```

Reverse.

```
1. 𒀭 𒀜
   𒁴𒐈
3. 𒁴𒐈 𒁴
   𒌋𒌍 𒁴
   𒈹 𒁴 𒀭
6. 𒀜 𒀭𒁹 𒍑
   𒈹 𒀭 𒌋𒌋
   𒈹 𒀜 𒁹
9. 𒍑 𒀭𒐈 𒀭𒐈 𒌋𒌋
```

[936.] K. 13006.

OBVERSE.

(cuneiform text, 7 lines, partly defaced)

3.

REVERSE.

(cuneiform text, partly defaced)

3.

6.

9.

EDGE.

[1] Defaced.

OBVERSE.

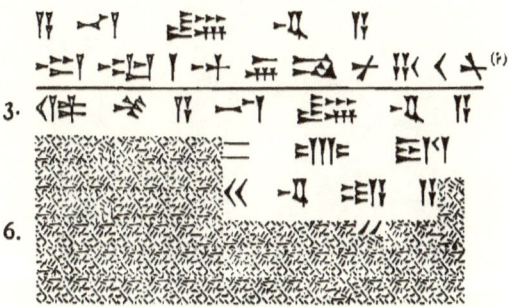

3.

6.

REVERSE completely broken away.

OBVERSE.

1.

3.

6.

9.

REVERSE not inscribed.

[939.] **K. 13094.**

OBVERSE.

𒅁𒄩𒂍𒀴𒐕
𒂍𒅁𒀭𒁺𒌋𒌋𒌍

3. 𒂍𒀪𒐊𒅁𒄩𒂍𒀴𒐕
𒐕𒂍𒀴𒐕𒐊𒐊𒅁𒐕
𒐕𒁺𒋗𒂍𒂍

6. 𒐕𒐕𒐕𒐕𒐕𒐕𒐕
𒀭𒐊𒁺𒌋𒂍𒐕𒐕
𒀭𒐊𒐕𒐕𒐕𒐕

REVERSE completely broken away.

[940.] Sm. 1428.

OBVERSE.

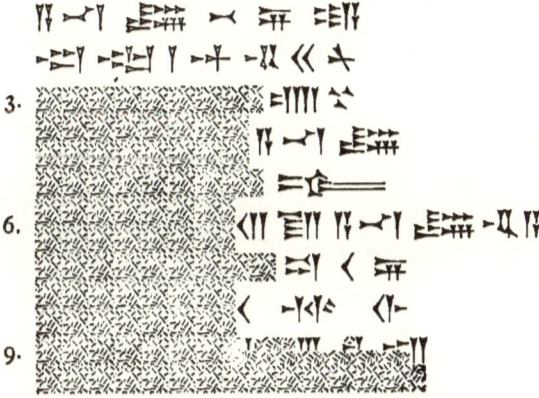

REVERSE.

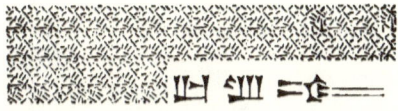

[941.]   82–5–22, 115.

OBVERSE.

3.

6.

REVERSE broken away.

[942.] 83–1–18, 71.

Obverse.

3.

6.

9.

12.

Reverse.

3.

6.

9.

12.

15. Edge.

[943.]   83–1–18, 72.

OBVERSE.

3.

6.

9.

12.

REVERSE.

[944.] 83-1-18, 85.

Obverse.

3.

6.

9.

12.

Reverse.

3.

6.

[945.]   83–1–18, 96.

OBVERSE.

REVERSE.

LEFT-HAND EDGE: part of one line erased.

[946.] 83-1-18, 103.

OBVERSE.

𒅆 𒀀𒇻 𒂊𒈦 𒈬 𒌋
𒊑 𒊑𒁉 𒀭 𒌋 𒅆 𒐏 𒊑 𒈦

3. 𒂍 𒐊 𒐏𒈬 𒊩 𒅆𒀀𒇻 𒂊𒈦 𒈬 𒌋𒊑
𒐏𒈬 𒊩 𒅆𒀀𒇻 𒌋 𒌋𒁉 𒂊 𒌋 𒆷
𒈬𒅆 𒂊𒈦 𒈬 𒌋

6. 𒈨𒌍 𒌋𒁉 𒂊 𒆷 𒌋𒋻
𒅆 𒂊𒋻 𒌋𒁉 𒂊 𒆷
𒐏𒈬 𒊩 𒌋𒐉 𒂊𒈦

9. 𒌍 𒂍𒐊

REVERSE.

𒐏𒈬 𒐏 𒅆𒀀𒇻 𒅆 𒈦

3. 𒂊𒈦 𒈬 𒌋
𒅆𒁉 𒌋𒌋𒁉𒌋 𒂊𒈦 𒁁 𒊑𒀀𒇻
𒊩 𒐊𒊑 𒐊 𒐊 𒌋𒍣 𒌋𒌍 𒊑𒐊

6. 𒈦𒌋 𒌋𒌍 𒊩
𒂊𒈦 𒁁 𒊑𒀀𒇻 𒅆 𒀀𒇻 𒊑𒁉 𒌋
𒊑𒊑𒁉 𒌋𒁉 𒐊 𒊑𒐊

9. 𒂍 𒈨𒌍 𒅆 𒈦 𒊑𒐊 𒈦

6 Q

[947.] 83–1–18, 105.

OBVERSE.

〔cuneiform text〕

3. 〔cuneiform text〕

6. 〔cuneiform text〕

REVERSE.

〔cuneiform text〕

3. 〔cuneiform text〕

6. 〔cuneiform text〕

EDGE.

9. 〔cuneiform text〕

LEFT-HAND EDGE.

〔cuneiform text〕

12. 〔cuneiform text〕

[948.]   83-1-18, 111.

OBVERSE.

3.

6.

REVERSE.

3.

6.

EDGE.

9.

[949.] 83-1-18, 112.

Obverse.

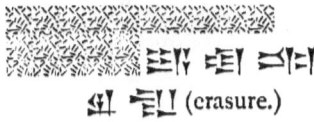

Reverse.

(crasure.)

[950.] 83–1–18, 155.

Obverse.

𒁹𒈨 𒈨𒌋 𒈨 𒈨𒌋 𒈨 𒈨𒌋

3. 𒈨 𒈨 𒈨 𒈨𒌋 𒈨 𒈨 𒈨 𒈨𒌋

6. 𒈨 𒈨 𒈨 𒈨 𒈨𒌋

Reverse.

𒈨𒌋 𒈨 𒈨 𒈨 𒈨𒌋 𒈨

3. 𒈨 𒈨 𒈨𒌋 𒈨 𒈨 𒈨

6. 𒈨 𒈨 𒈨 𒈨 𒈨 𒈨𒌋

[951.] **K. 189.**

Obverse.

3.

6.

9.

12.

15.

[951.] **K. 189** (*continued*).

OBVERSE.

¹ Defaced, and hence doubtful.

[951.] **K. 189** (*continued*).

REVERSE.

3.

6.

9.

12.

15.

[1] Division marks.   [2] Defaced, and hence doubtful.

[951.] **K. 189** (*continued*).

REVERSE.

18.

21.

24.

27.

EDGE.

LEFT-HAND EDGE.

30.

33.

[1] Traces of illegible signs. [2] Rubbed, and hence doubtful.

[952.] **K. 847.**

OBVERSE.

〔cuneiform text〕

3. 〔cuneiform text〕

6. 〔cuneiform text〕

9 〔cuneiform text〕

REVERSE.

〔cuneiform text〕

3. 〔cuneiform text〕

6. 〔cuneiform text〕

[953.] K. 892.

OBVERSE.

3.

6.

9.

12.

REVERSE.

3.

[954.] K. 895.

OBVERSE.

3.

6.

9.

12.

15.

[954.]   **K. 895** *(continued).*

REVERSE.

[955.] **K. 925.**

OBVERSE.

No REVERSE.

[956.] K. 930.

OBVERSE.

3.

6.

9.

12.

EDGE.

REVERSE.

3.

6.

9.

12.

15.

[957.] K. 932.

OBVERSE.

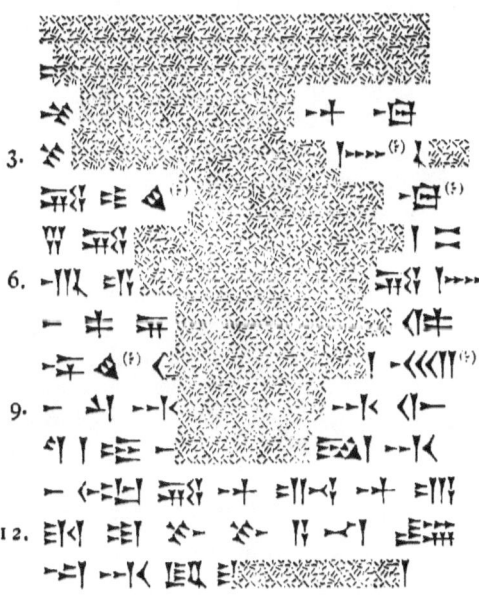

REVERSE.

OBVERSE.

[958.] **K. 1459** (*continued*).

REVERSE.

3.

6.

9.

12.

15.

18.

21.

EDGE.

24.

[959.] K. 1554.

OBVERSE.

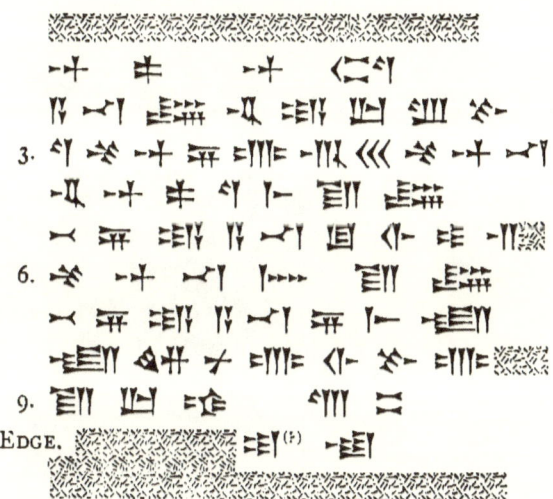

LEFT-HAND EDGE.

REVERSE broken away.

[960.] K. 1580.

OBVERSE.

3.

6.

9.

12.

15.

EDGE.

18.

[960.] **K. 1580** (*continued*).

REVERSE.

𒀭𒀭𒀭𒀭𒀭𒀭 𒀭𒀭𒀭𒀭𒀭 𒀭𒀭𒀭𒀭𒀭(¹) 𒀭𒀭𒀭 𒀭
𒀭𒀭𒀭𒀭𒀭 𒀭𒀭 𒀭𒀭 𒀭𒀭 𒀭𒀭𒀭 𒀭𒀭

3. 𒀭𒀭 𒀭𒀭 𒀭𒀭𒀭 𒀭𒀭𒀭 𒀭𒀭 𒀭𒀭 𒀭𒀭 𒀭𒀭
𒀭𒀭𒀭 𒀭𒀭 𒀭 𒀭𒀭 𒀭𒀭 𒀭 𒀭 𒀭𒀭 𒀭 𒀭𒀭 𒀭 𒀭 𒀭
𒀭𒀭 𒀭 𒀭 𒀭𒀭𒀭 𒀭 𒀭 𒀭𒀭 𒀭𒀭𒀭 𒀭𒀭𒀭 𒀭 𒀭

6. 𒀭𒀭 𒀭 𒀭 𒀭𒀭𒀭𒀭 𒀭 𒀭𒀭 𒀭𒀭 𒀭𒀭 𒀭𒀭𒀭 𒀭𒀭𒀭 𒀭 𒀭 𒀭
𒀭 𒀭𒀭𒀭 𒀭 𒀭𒀭 𒀭 𒀭 𒀭 𒀭𒀭𒀭 𒀭𒀭𒀭 𒀭 𒀭𒀭𒀭𒀭 𒀭
𒀭𒀭 𒀭 𒀭𒀭 𒀭𒀭𒀭 𒀭 𒀭 𒀭 𒀭 𒀭𒀭𒀭 𒀭𒀭 𒀭𒀭𒀭 𒀭 𒀭 𒀭

9. 𒀭 𒀭𒀭 𒀭𒀭 𒀭𒀭 𒀭 𒀭𒀭𒀭 𒀭 𒀭 𒀭 𒀭𒀭 𒀭 𒀭
𒀭𒀭𒀭 𒀭𒀭 𒀭𒀭𒀭 𒀭𒀭 𒀭𒀭 𒀭𒀭𒀭 𒀭 𒀭 𒀭 𒀭 𒀭𒀭
𒀭𒀭 𒀭𒀭𒀭 𒀭 𒀭 𒀭𒀭𒀭 𒀭𒀭𒀭 𒀭𒀭 𒀭 𒀭 𒀭𒀭𒀭 𒀭𒀭

12. 𒀭 𒀭𒀭𒀭 𒀭𒀭𒀭 𒀭 𒀭 𒀭
𒀭 𒀭 𒀭𒀭(⁵) 𒀭

[961.] K. 1610.

Obverse.

Reverse.

[962.] K. 1881.

OBVERSE.

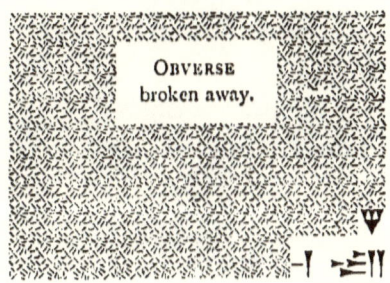

OBVERSE
broken away.

REVERSE.

3.

6.

9.

EDGE. 12.

LEFT-HAND EDGE.

(Erasure)

---

[1] First wedge of an unfinished sign.
[2] From OBVERSE.

[963.] K. 1895.

Obverse.

3.

6.

9.

12.

Reverse.

3.

6.

9.

12.

[964.] K. 2645.

OBVERSE.

（楔形文字）

3.

6.

9.

12.

15.

18.

[964.] **K. 2645** (*continued*).

REVERSE.

3.

6.

9.

12.

15.

18.

1 𒌋.

Obverse.

[965.] K. 2889 (*continued*).

18.

21.

24.

27.

Edge.

30.

33.

[965.] **K. 2889** (*continued*).

Reverse.

[965.] K. 2889 (*continued*).

REVERSE.

18.

21.

24.

27.

30.

[966.] K. 4724.

OBVERSE.

REVERSE.

[967.] K. 4776.

OBV.

3.

6.

9.

12.

REV.

3.

6.

9.

12.

15.

18.

LEFT-HAND
EDGE.

¹ Perhaps ⟨cuneiform⟩ written over an erasure.

[968.] K. 4789.

OBVERSE.

[968.] **K. 4789** (*continued*).

REVERSE.

[969.] K. 8671.

OBVERSE.

(cuneiform signs, lines 1–2)

3. *(cuneiform signs)*

(cuneiform signs)

(cuneiform signs)

6. *(cuneiform signs)*

(cuneiform signs)

(cuneiform signs)

9. *(cuneiform signs)*

(cuneiform signs)

(cuneiform signs)

12. *(cuneiform signs)*

(cuneiform signs)

REVERSE.

(cuneiform signs)

[970.] 83–1–18, 50.

Obverse.

3.

6.

9.

Reverse.

3.

6.

9.

[971.]   83-1-18, 54.

OBVERSE.

3.

6.

9.

EDGE.

12.

REVERSE.

3.

6.

[972.] 83-1-18, 59.

Obverse.

3.

6.

9.

Edge.

12.

Reverse.

3.

6.

9.

[1] Written over an erasure and hence doubtful.

OBVERSE.

𒀭𒌋 𒑱𒑱𒑱𒑱𒑱𒑱𒑱𒑱𒑱𒑱𒑱

𒆠 𒌷 𒂍𒈨 𒊬 𒐼 𒀸

3. 𒐊 𒌍 𒂊𒌈 𒊹 𒂍𒈨 𒐊𒈨 𒂍 𒌷 𒐊 𒐊

𒂍𒈨 𒂊𒋻 𒐽 𒂍𒐊𒐊 𒂍𒀸

𒀪 𒂊𒌈 𒊹 𒂍𒈨 𒐊𒈨 𒂍 𒌷 𒐊 𒐊

6. 𒂍𒈨 𒂊𒋻 𒀖 𒀉𒊬 𒂍𒈨 𒀀𒈨 𒂍𒊏

𒀪 𒂊𒌈 𒊹 𒂍𒈨 𒐊𒈨 𒂍 𒌷 𒐊 𒐊

𒂍𒈨 𒐊 𒀪 𒀖 𒈫 𒂊𒈨 𒂊𒋻 𒀪 𒀉

9. 𒋻 𒐊 𒌍 𒑱𒑱 𒂊𒌈 𒊹 𒂍𒈨 𒐊𒈨

𒂍 𒌷 𒐊 𒐊 𒂍𒈨 𒌷𒑱

EDGE.

𒀉 𒊬 𒀭𒌋 𒌷 𒂍𒑱𒑱𒈨

12. 𒀉𒊬 𒊬 𒊬 𒌋 𒌷

REVERSE completely broken away.

[974.]   83–1–18, 99.

OBVERSE.

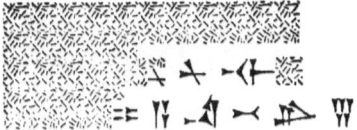

3.

6.

9.

EDGE.

12.

REVERSE.

3.

6.

LEFT-HAND EDGE.

9.

INDEX I.

z

SCRIBE	NO.	KOUYUNJIK NO.	PAGE
	926	K. 4447	1001
	927	K. 4522	1002
	928	K. 5463	1003
	929	K. 5496	1004
	930	K. 5607	1005
	931	K. 7370	1006
	932	K. 7487	1007
	933	K. 8855	1008
	934	K. 12953	1009
	935	K. 12969	1010
	936	K. 13006	1011
	937	K. 13030	1012
	938	S. 1201	1013
	939	K. 13094	1014
	940	S. 1428	1015
	941	82-5-22, 115	1016
	942	83-1-18, 71	1017
	943	83-1-18, 72	1018
	944	83-1-18, 85	1019
	945	83-1-18, 96	1020
	946	83-1-18, 103	1021
	947	83-1-18, 105	1022
	948	83-1-18, 111	1023
	949	83-1-18, 112	1024
	950	83-1-18, 155	1025
	951	K. 189	1026-1029
	952	K. 847	1030

s 2

SCRIBE	NO.	KOUYUNJIK NO.	PAGE
	953	K. 892	1031
	954	K. 895	1032, 1033
	955	K. 925	1034
	956	K. 930	1035
	957	K. 932	1036
	958	K. 1459	1037, 1038
	959	K. 1554	1039
	960	K. 1580	1040, 1041
	961	K. 1610	1042
	962	K. 1881	1043
	963	K. 1895	1044
	964	K. 2645	1045, 1046
	965	K. 2889	1047–1050
	966	K. 4724	1051
	967	K. 4776	1052
	968	K. 4789	1053, 1054
	969	K. 8671	1055
	970	83-1-18, 50	1056
	971	83-1-18, 54	1057
	972	83-1-18, 59	1058
	973	83-1-18, 97	1059
	974	83-1-18, 99	1060

INDEX II.

INDEX III.

A List of Tablets published in Parts I-IX.

www.ingramcontent.com/pod-product-compliance
Lightning Source LLC
Chambersburg PA
CBHW031347020726
47499CB00005B/1437